One More Spot

This story shows that the best reward for doing a good deed is the special feeling you get inside.

Story by:
Michelle Baron

Illustrated by:
David High
Russell Hicks
Theresa Mazurek
Allyn Conley/Gorniak
Julie Ann Armstrong

WORLDS OF WONDER

Grubby™   Newton Gimmick™   Princess Aruzia™   Leota™   Wooly What's-It™   Fobs™

Prince Arin™

Today the sun is shining brightly.

Page 1

We landed the Airship
and unloaded our picnic.

Would you like to come to the Bug Fair?

Gimmick got the Portable Reducing Machine and pushed the red button.

There was so much to see at the Fair.

Amanda took us to the Bug Circus, where we saw all kinds of wonderful circus acts.

Then the bug Master
of Ceremonies started
awarding spots.